Beauty and the Beast

For Adèle Geras

Cinderella • Kaye Umansky
The Christmas Story • David Wood

Published 1996 by
A & C Black (Publishers) Limited
35 Bedford Row, London WC1R 4JH

ISBN 0-7136-4390-0

A CIP catalogue record for this book is available from the British Library.

Series Advisor: Prue Goodwin,
Reading and Language Information Centre,
University of Reading

Photoset in New Century Schoolbook.

Printed in Great Britain by
Hillman Printers (Frome) Ltd, Frome, Somerset.

Performance
For permission to give a public performance of **Beauty and the Beast** at which an admission charge is made, please write to MLR, 200 Fulham Road, London SW10 9PN. You do not need permission if you do not plan to charge an entry fee for the performance.

Beauty and the Beast

Jacqueline Wilson

Illustrated by Peter Kavanagh

A & C BLACK • LONDON

Contents

1. A Letter from the Playwright 5

2. Characters in Order of Appearance 6

3. List of Scenes and their Locations 6

4. Beauty and the Beast – the Play 7

5. Director's Notes:

1. Staging 36

2. Scenery and Props 37

3. Lighting 40

4. Casting and Auditions 40

5. The Main Characters 42

6. The Stage Management Team 44

7. Costume 45

8. Music 48

9. Dances 48

10. Sound Effects 48

11. Anything Else? 48

A Letter from the Playwright

I always fancied myself as an actress when I was a little girl. I performed all the parts in endless imaginary plays at home and I mumbled and grimaced dramatically as I walked to and fro from school. (People must have backed away rapidly when they saw me coming!) I was very excited when our teacher told us we were going to put on a play of 'The Sleeping Beauty'. I'd read the story but somehow I still managed to get hold of the wrong end of the stick when I was chosen to be the Queen. I thought I'd been picked for the star part. I was disappointed when I realised I was only Sleeping Beauty's mum – and I had precisely one line to say.

I still adored being involved in the production of that play. I loved the joky rehearsals, the dressing up, the heady excitement as the hall filled with the other children and a few supportive parents. Our audience! I didn't suffer from stage fright. I sat in a queenly fashion on a school chair throne, waving my toy sceptre regally and tipping my cardboard crown at a fetching angle. There was a sudden silence on stage. Someone's forgotten their words, I thought. The silence stretched on alarmingly. It was a very long time before I realised something. I was the someone.

Perhaps it's just as well that I became a writer rather than an actress! I had great fun writing *Beauty and the Beast*. I hope you and the children will enjoy yourselves too, whether you're reading the play together or putting on a performance. You might be lucky enough to have a proper stage with curtains, theatrical lighting, a trunk of wondrous costumes, enthusiastic colleagues, helpful skilled parents, and a class of brilliant little thespians. Well, then you won't need to consult the Director's Notes! On the other hand, maybe you've got no resources whatsoever, just a classroom and a bunch of ordinary, messing-about, fidgety kids who have never performed in a play before. If so, maybe some of the suggestions at the back of this book will be useful.

Happy acting!

Characters in Order of Appearance

Bushes (a minimum of eight)
Marble Statue
Beauty
Grace
Melody
Merchant
Gate (two actors)

Willing Hands: One
Two
Three
Four
Five
Six

Beast

List of Scenes and their Locations

Act 1

Scene 1 – Beauty and her Sisters	: *Beauty's Garden*
Scene 2 – A Wild Night	: *Outside the Palace*
Scene 3 – Strange Meetings	: *The Rose Garden*
Scene 4 – The Merchant's Bargain	: *Beauty's Garden*

[Interval if desired]

Act 2

Scene 1 – An Introduction	: *Outside the Palace*
Scene 2 – An Offer of Marriage	: *The Rose Garden*
Scene 3 – Home Once More	: *The Merchant's Bedroom*
Scene 4 – Love Conquers All	: *The Rose Garden*

The playing time is approximately 45 minutes without an interval.

Act 1, Scene 1 - Beauty and her Sisters

Beauty's Garden. The BUSHES stand in a semi-circle.
The MARBLE STATUE sits in the centre on a small plinth.
The BUSHES chant the following lines in turn.

BUSHES: I am lilac
I am lime
I am lavender
I am thyme
I am hydrangea
I am heather

(All together) We stand here
In the garden
Whatever the weather

I am fuchsia
I am gorse
I am delicate
I am coarse
I am so pretty
I'm good to eat
I am the tallest
(Jostling) I am the tallest
No, I'm the tallest
I smell so sweet.

(Light shines on the MARBLE STATUE.)

MARBLE STATUE: Not as sweet as a rose though.
(to the audience)
I am Cupid. Finest marble.
I wish Beauty had more luck growing roses.
They'd set me off a treat.

TWO BUSHES: *(sadly)* We're not roses.

TWO MORE BUSHES: *(sadly)* We don't have posies.

(Footsteps are heard approaching.)

MARBLE STATUE: Shush, bush!

(BEAUTY comes on stage with a trowel and a water spray. She sprays several of the BUSHES, making them squeal. She puts down the trowel and the water spray, then bends down to examine a small dead rose bush.)

MARBLE STATUE: *(whispers to audience)* All Beauty's roses get eaten by...

BEAUTY: *(screams)* Aaaaaaaaah! Slugs! Ugh! I can't stand slugs!

(GRACE and MELODY enter the garden. They sigh impatiently at BEAUTY.)

GRACE: What are you screaming about now?

BEAUTY: There was this slug.

MELODY: Oh, you're such a baby! Imagine being scared of a slug.

GRACE: *(picking up the trowel)* Sluggies are nice little friendies, Beauty. Come and make friends with the sluggy.

MELODY: *(grabbing the trowel)* Yes, down the neck of your dressy!

(BEAUTY starts to run away. She bumps into the MERCHANT, as he enters.)

MERCHANT: What's all the shrieking for?

GRACE: Oh, it's just Beauty being silly again, Father.

MELODY: You know how she always makes a fuss.

BEAUTY: *(shuddering)* Slugs!

MERCHANT: Oh Beauty! Slugs can't hurt you.
Now calm down, girls. I want you to be very good.
I've got to go to town on business.

GRACE: Will you bring us back a present, Father?

MELODY: Yes, then we'll be really good.

MERCHANT: But my darlings, we've so little money left now.

GRACE: Oh Father, I've got to have new dancing shoes. Look, my toes are peeping straight through.

MELODY: And I must have a flute, Father, it's not fair I've only got a silly penny whistle.

MERCHANT: All right, all right, I'll do my best, girls. A pair of dancing shoes for Grace. And a flute for Melody.

GRACE: Glass slippers, Father. Satin wears out in weeks.

MELODY: Silver flutes sound much sweeter than plain old wood.

MERCHANT: What about you, Beauty? What present would you like?

BEAUTY: Oh, it doesn't matter, Father. I don't really need anything!

MERCHANT: Come on, Beauty. Surely there's something you'd like?

BEAUTY: Well. . . No, it sounds so silly.

MERCHANT: *(fondly)* Tell me.

BEAUTY: *(shyly)* I'd like a rose in bloom.

GRACE and MELODY: *(together)* It's silly all right.

MERCHANT: A rose in bloom. Your mother was always so fond of roses, Beauty. Sometimes you remind me of her so much. . .

(The MERCHANT exits sadly.)

GRACE: *(to BEAUTY)* There. Now you've upset Father.

MELODY: *(to BEAUTY)* Typical!

GRACE: *(running after MERCHANT)* Father, you won't forget my dancing shoes?

MELODY: Or my flute?

(MELODY and GRACE exit.)

BEAUTY: Oh dear. Poor Father. I didn't mean to make him unhappy.

(The BUSHES, BEAUTY and the MARBLE STATUE exit.)

Act 1, Scene 2 - A Wild Night

Outside the Palace. There is a GATE represented by two actors who stand centre stage. It is a stormy night, with frequent thunder and lightning. There is the sound of a horse neighing and the rapid clip-clop of hooves.

The MERCHANT enters, looking dishevelled.

MERCHANT: Where did that wretched horse go?
The lightning made him bolt and I toppled straight off.
Oh, my shoulder! And my leg!
I'll have to get help.
(Looks around desperately.)
But I'm lost in the wood.
And it's such a terrible night.

(More thunder.)

MERCHANT: I'd better try to keep moving.
Maybe there will be a woodcutter's cottage
or a little hut where I can find shelter.

(He blunders around the stage hopelessly.)

MERCHANT: I can't go on. My leg hurts so.
I've lost the dancing slippers and the silver flute
and the rose bush for my Beauty.
Oh, how I wish I was safe at home!

(The MERCHANT falls down in front of the GATE. He looks up, sees it and touches it. He tries to open the GATE and fails.)

MERCHANT: Locked! If only I had a key.

(ONE comes on stage, holding a large key.)

ONE: Here is a key, Honoured Guest.

(The MERCHANT jumps. He takes the key very gingerly.)

MERCHANT: I think I'm dreaming!
But I may as well see if the key turns.

(The MERCHANT mimes the action of putting the key in the GATE. He turns the key. TWO enters and bobs up on the other side of the GATE.)

TWO: Please enter the enchanted garden, Honoured Guest.

MERCHANT: *(nervously)* Thank you. Thank you.

(THREE, FOUR and FIVE rush on stage, miming holding up lanterns.)

THREE, FOUR, FIVE: Allow us to light your way, Honoured Guest.

(All the WILLING HANDS help the MERCHANT towards the edge of the stage.)

MERCHANT: It <u>must</u> be a dream.

(The MERCHANT puts out a hand as if to knock at a door, then hesitates.)

ONE: Yes, knock at the door, Honoured Guest.
Enter the enchanted palace.

MERCHANT: Whose guest am I?

TWO: Our Master's, Honoured Guest.

MERCHANT: And who <u>is</u> your master?

THREE, FOUR, FIVE: He whom we serve, Honoured Guest.

MERCHANT: Yes, but. . . Oh, this is ridiculous.
Thank you kindly, er... Willing Hands.

(The MERCHANT goes off stage. The WILLING HANDS wave goodbye to him. As he goes, SIX rushes on stage.)

SIX: Where's the honoured guest?

ONE: *(sighing)* You've missed him.

SIX: Has he met *(lowers voice)* our Master?

ONE: Not yet. . .

(A loud thunderclap is heard. All exit.)

Act 1, Scene 3 - Strange Meetings

The Rose Garden. It is morning. The BUSHES stand in a semi-circle, and link arms to form a hedge. The MERCHANT enters, very spruce and smart.

MERCHANT: What a wonderful smell!

BUSHES: *(swaying, pleased with themselves)* We are roses, holding posies. We are roses, holding posies.

MERCHANT: Beautiful roses in full bloom. There are so many flowers in the palace gardens. But these roses are the best of all. I thought the lotion in my morning bath had a lovely smell – it soothed away all my aches and pains – but it's nothing compared to these roses.

BUSHES: We are roses, holding posies.
Beautiful roses holding beautiful posies.

MERCHANT: How my little Beauty would love to walk in this rose bower. She wanted a rose in bloom.
I've lost the dancing slippers, I've lost the silver flute – but I could pick just one rose and take it home for Beauty.

(The MERCHANT reaches out. The BUSHES look shocked. Strange tinkling music sounds, from off stage.)

MERCHANT: I suppose I ought to ask permission. But I haven't seen the mysterious master of this castle yet.
I thought we would meet at breakfast.
(licking lips) Such a delightful meal,
served by those very Willing Hands.
I know! I'll ask the Hands to pick me a rose.
(raises voice) Willing Hands?

(WILLING HANDS ONE, TWO, THREE, FOUR and FIVE come on stage very rapidly.)

ONE: What do you desire, Honoured Guest?

MERCHANT: Pick me a rose, please.

(All the WILLING HANDS spread their fingers wide in shock and then clench their hands into fists.)

MERCHANT: *(turning to TWO)* Just one?

(TWO clenches his fists again.)

MERCHANT: *(turning to THREE, FOUR and FIVE)* Please?

(THREE, FOUR AND FIVE clench their fists again.)

MERCHANT: Won't <u>any</u> of you help me?

(SIX rushes on stage.)

SIX: *(breathlessly)* What do you desire, Honoured Guest?

MERCHANT: Just one rose. It would mean so much to my youngest daughter.

(SIX clenches his hands into fists.)

MERCHANT: If you won't – I will!

(The MERCHANT reaches out and plucks the rose. The music is heard again, louder than before. The BUSHES draw breath, horrified.)

BUSHES: Oooooooooh, Oooooooooh, Oooooooooh!

(The BEAST slides on to the stage.)

MERCHANT: *(screams)* Whatever is i-i-i-i-i-i-i-i-t!
(cowering) A slug! A gigantic monstrous beastly s-l-u-u-u-g!

BEAST: And <u>you</u> are a common thief!

MERCHANT: No, I –

BEAST: A thief who creeps into my private garden and steals my finest roses.

MERCHANT: One rose.

BEAST: Yet I have given you every hospitality!
My Willing Hands have flexed their fingers
night and day on your behalf.

MERCHANT: Your Willing Hands? So you are the Master?
A vast slimy slug?

BEAST: You not only steal my roses, you insult my person.
I take great care not to be slimy.

(The BEAST looks over to the WILLING HANDS. They flutter about the BEAST and mime the action of patting the BEAST dry with cloths.)

BEAST: *(as they do this)* There are no two ways about this.
You will die for your impertinence.
(threateningly) Willing Hands!
Seize him!

(The MERCHANT flings himself down on his knees. WILLING HANDS ONE, TWO, THREE, FOUR and FIVE hold him tightly. SIX tries to pat the MERCHANT comfortingly.)

MERCHANT: Have mercy, Great Slug. Beast. Master!

BEAST: Why did you steal this rose when there were
vast bouquets in your bedroom, overflowing
vases in every room?

MERCHANT: Not roses. Every flower, but not roses.

BEAST: Do you particularly care for roses?
They are my favourites too.

MERCHANT: Yes! Yes, I do – but this rose wasn't for me.
It was to be a gift for my youngest daughter.
She loves roses so much.

BEAST: Then why can't she grow her own?

MERCHANT: Beauty's tried and tried, but the slu. . .
She's always failed.

BEAST: She's called Beauty, this daughter of yours?

MERCHANT: I have three daughters. Grace, Melody and Beauty.

BEAST: Is Grace graceful?

MERCHANT: Very graceful.

(The BUSHES sway gracefully.)

BEAST: Is Melody melodious?

MERCHANT: Very melodious.

(The BUSHES sing to the tune of Lavender's Blue.)

BUSHES: *Roses are red, dilly dilly*
Roses are yellow
Melody sings, dilly dilly
With voice sweet and mellow.

BEAST: And is Beauty. . . beautiful?

MERCHANT: Beauty is the most beautiful girl in all the land
– even more beautiful than your rose garden, Sir.

BEAST: Then take the rose to your youngest daughter
Beauty, Merchant.
(gestures to WILLING HANDS) Unhand him!
(to MERCHANT) I will provide you with a horse.
He will take you to your home.

(The WILLING HANDS let the MERCHANT go. He starts to back away from the BEAST.)

MERCHANT: Thank you, thank you so much, Sir, Master...

BEAST: (ominously) But -

(The BUSHES freeze.)

BEAST:	But when the rose petals start to fall, your youngest daughter Beauty must come to meet me.

(The BUSHES droop.)

MERCHANT:	Not Beauty!
BEAST:	She must mount the horse and come here to my palace. Now Merchant, be gone before I change my mind!
MERCHANT:	But I can't let Beauty –
BEAST:	You will do as I say, or –
ONE:	Go!
TWO:	Go!
THREE, FOUR, FIVE:	Go, go, go!
SIX:	*(desperately)* Go!

(The MERCHANT runs off stage. All the others exit.)

Act 1, Scene 4 – The Merchant's Bargain

Beauty's Garden. The MARBLE STATUE stands on his plinth. The MERCHANT is stooped beneath the MARBLE STATUE. GRACE, MELODY and BEAUTY are standing close to him. BEAUTY has the half-dead rose in a vase.

MARBLE STATUE: *(to audience)* The Merchant returned with the rose.
He told the tale of the loathsome Beast
and the terrible bargain he had made.

MERCHANT: But you can't go, Beauty.

BEAUTY: I have to go, Father. The rose is fading.
And you are getting ill. It must be the Beast's doing.
I have to keep to his bargain.
I must go to his enchanted palace.

MERCHANT: I won't let you.

BEAUTY: I have to go. Farewell, dearest Father.
(She kisses him.)
Goodbye, Grace, goodbye Melody.
You will look after Father, won't you?

GRACE: Oh, Beauty! You will be all right?

MELODY: Maybe the Beast just wants to look at you?

GRACE: If you only hadn't asked for that stupid rose.

MELODY: You should have asked for slippers or a flute.
Even though we didn't get them.

(BEAUTY runs off, but she stops at the corner of the stage.)

BEAUTY: Oh dear, I'm so scared. But I've got to go, for Father's sake.
And maybe – maybe the Beast won't be too frightening. . .

(BEAUTY exits.)

MARBLE STATUE: *(peering down helplessly from his plinth)* Isn't anyone going to stop her?

GRACE: Never mind, Father, you've still got us.

MELODY: Yes, don't take on so.

MERCHANT: *(weakly)* I couldn't bear to describe the Beast to Beauty. . .

(All exit.)

INTERVAL

Act 2, Scene 1 – An Introduction

Outside the Palace. We can hear a horse neighing off stage. BEAUTY enters and creeps up to the GATE.

BEAUTY: *(whispering)* This must be the gate
to the enchanted palace.
(She tries to open it.) It's locked.
I don't really want to get in.
But I must try to be brave. I shall go to meet
this Beast and thank him for the rose.
Maybe he'll take pity on me and let me go home again.
And Father will recover and we'll live happily ever after.
(taking deep breath) So I need to find the key
to the gate first.

(WILLING HANDS ONE, TWO, THREE, FOUR and FIVE enter. ONE is holding the key. BEAUTY jumps.)

BEAUTY: Ah! You must be the Willing Hands.
My father spoke warmly of you.

ONE: We are more than willing for you, Beauty.

TWO: *(grabbing the key from ONE)* Here is the key.

BEAUTY: Thank you very much.

(She takes it and tries to turn it. SIX enters.)

SIX: Oh! She must be Beauty. She's beautiful.

ONE: Please, allow us, Beauty.

TWO: Such a tiny hand!

THREE, FOUR, FIVE: Let us help you through the gate, Beauty.

SIX: *(desperately eager)* Could we be of any help at all, Beauty?

(There is the sound of a horse neighing, off stage.)

ONE: Some Willing Hands should stable the horse!

TWO: We're helping Beauty.

THREE, FOUR, FIVE: So are we.

ONE: *(as the key turns and the GATE is opened)*
Please enter our enchanted garden, Beauty.

(BEAUTY goes through the GATE, while WILLING HANDS ONE, TWO, THREE, FOUR and FIVE follow.)

(There is the sound of a horse neighing again.)

SIX: It's not fair. We hate stabling the horse!

(SIX goes off stage. BEAUTY is led by the other WILLING HANDS towards the side of the stage.)

ONE: This way, Beauty.

TWO: Such dainty hands, Beauty.

THREE, FOUR, FIVE: Can we hold your hand, Beauty?

(ONE elbows them all out of the way and takes BEAUTY's hand.)

BEAUTY: You're all being so kind to me.
I was silly to be so scared of coming here.
I'm sure your Master's very kind, isn't he?
Even if he looks a little strange?

*(The WILLING HANDS wriggle their fingers nervously.
BEAUTY and the WILLING HANDS all approach an imaginary door.
BEAUTY puts her hand on an imaginary knocker - and then hesitates.)*

ONE: Yes, knock at the door, Beauty.
Enter the enchanted palace.

BEAUTY:	Does your Master know I'm here?
ONE:	Oh indeed yes, Beauty. We have been scrubbing and shaking –
TWO:	Brewing and baking –
THREE:	Preparing a feast –
FOUR:	For our Master the Beast –
FIVE:	And his beautiful Beauty –
SIX:	*(rushing on stage)* We have all done our duty.
BEAUTY:	And I will do my duty too. I will go and meet your Master.

(BEAUTY knocks at an imaginary door at the side of the stage.)

BEAUTY:	*(whispers)* I mustn't be scared. He can't help the way he looks. I probably shan't mind at all. And he's gone to so much trouble.

(BEAUTY opens the imaginary door and looks out.)

BEAUTY:	Good evening? I am Beauty.

(The BEAST slimes dramatically on stage towards her.)

BEAST:	And I am the Beast.
BEAUTY:	*(screams)* Aaaaaaaaaaaaaah!

(All exit.)

Act 2, Scene 2 – An Offer of Marriage

The Rose Garden. It is evening. The BUSHES sit in a semi-circle. BEAUTY rushes on stage.

BEAUTY: His face! His feelers! His slugginess! His slime!

(WILLING HANDS ONE, TWO, THREE, FOUR, FIVE and SIX follow BEAUTY. ONE is holding a hankie and TWO is holding an envelope.)

BEAUTY: *(terrified)* Is he coming?

ONE: No, No! Compose yourself, Beauty.
(ONE gives her the hankie.)

BEAUTY: Thank you. *(She mops and blows her nose daintily.)*

ONE: Do try not mention the 's' words. . .
(whispers) s-l-u-g and indeed s-l-i-m-e.
Our Master is very sensitive to these specific matters – and he has very sharp ears.

TWO: *(holding out an envelope)* Our Master sends you a message, Beauty.

(BEAUTY opens the envelope and reads the letter aloud.)

BEAUTY: Dear Beauty, I am sorry our first meeting was so short.
Please return to the dining room and refresh yourself.
I will eat in my room tonight as I see you are a little nervous of conversation. Adieu until tomorrow.
Grand Beast, Lord and Master.
(gasping) Ooh!

ONE: Do as our Master bids, Beauty.

TWO: It really is an absolutely wonderful feast, Beauty.

ONE: It would be such a shame to waste it.
(Lowers voice.) Don't worry. We really did see Master retire to his room. You'll be all alone, Beauty.

THREE, FOUR, FIVE: Except for us, Beauty.

SIX: All of us, Beauty. Willing Hands at your command.

(The WILLING HANDS start to help BEAUTY off the stage.)

ONE: I think you will find your bedroom suite satisfactory, Beauty.

TWO: Wait till you see the dresses in your wardrobe – all in your specially tiny size.

THREE: Yes, you'll like trying on all your dresses.

FOUR: We like the pink best.

FIVE: No, the silver sparkles is much prettier.

ONE: And there's an art gallery full of your favourite paintings, Beauty.

TWO: And a library of all your favourite books.

(BEAUTY and WILLING HANDS ONE, TWO, THREE, FOUR and FIVE exit.)

SIX: *(capering after them)* Yes, wait till you see everything, Beauty. You'll soon cheer up!

(SIX exits.)

(The lights darken – and then brighten again. As the BUSHES sing to the tune of Lavender's Blue, SIX enters.)

BUSHES: *Roses are red, dilly dilly,*
Night time is dark
Beauty sleeps soft, dilly dilly
And is up with the lark.

SIX: Where are they? They've all gone off without me. . . again!

(BEAUTY enters, attended by ONE, TWO, THREE, FOUR and FIVE.)

SIX: *(delightedly)* There you are, Beauty.
How can we serve you now?

BEAUTY: I feel as if I am the Queen of this enchanted palace!

(The BEAST enters.)

BEAST: And I am the King!

(BEAUTY shudders and cowers.)

BEAST: Again?

BEAUTY: I – I am sorry, Sir. I. . .

(BEAUTY covers her eyes.)

BEAST: Can't you even look at me?

BEAUTY: No!

BEAST: Am I so very loathsome?

(BEAUTY swallows, unable to answer.)

BEAST: Willing Hands, quick! Deslime!

(All six WILLING HANDS mime wiping the BEAST dry.)

BEAST: There!

(BEAUTY takes one peep and flinches.)

BEAST: Look, I'm not going to hurt you, girl.
Nothing could be further from my mind!

BEAUTY: You tried to hurt my father, Sir.

BEAST: I was merely. . . warning him.

(The BUSHES whisper to each other.)

BEAST: I needed to frighten him a little
– so that you would come here.

BEAUTY: Well. I am here. What do you want of me, Sir?

BEAST: You are the most beautiful girl in all the land.

BEAUTY: Oh, I'm not!

BEAST: Modest too! Well, Beauty. I. . . I want you to marry me.

BEAUTY: *(amazed)* Marry you?

BEAST: I know my appearance disturbs you a little.
Perhaps it's asking too much for you to fall in
love with me.

BEAUTY: *(faintly)* In love. . . with you?

BEAST: I am exceedingly wealthy, with many willing servants.
All I am suggesting is a marriage of convenience.

BEAUTY: Never!

BEAST: You should try to get to know me a little better.
(He approaches her.)
I wish you wouldn't flinch so!

BEAUTY: I am sorry, Sir. I don't wish to offend you.
But I would have to love you if I agreed to marry you.
I'll never love you!

BEAST: We shall see!

(The BEAST exits grandly in a huff, with the WILLING HANDS. The BUSHES sing to the tune of Lavender's Blue.)

BUSHES: *Roses are red, dilly dilly*
The Beast's heart is too
He'll woo her with gifts, dilly dilly
So she'll say I do.

BEAUTY: I won't!

(WILLING HANDS ONE, TWO, THREE, FOUR and FIVE enter. THREE, FOUR and FIVE are carrying a book, a fan, and a piece of jewellery.)

ONE: Our Master courted Beauty from a distance.

TWO: He laid on a feast every night.

THREE, FOUR, FIVE: He gave her wonderful presents.

(WILLING HANDS THREE, FOUR and FIVE give their presents to BEAUTY. Enter BEAST with SIX running along behind him, covering him with a cloak.)

SIX: *(to audience)* He hid his sliminess under a cloak
so Beauty could stand his presence.

BEAST: Are you getting to like me just a little, Beauty?

BEAUTY: Well, you've been very kind, Sir.

(The BEAST is thrilled. He leaps up and moves nearer to BEAUTY. BEAUTY hides her face.)

BEAUTY: But I can never marry you, Beast.

(The BEAST despairs.)

ONE: But the Beast continued to woo Beauty.

(The BEAST flaps the edges of his cloak as if they are wings.)

BEAST: *(imitating an owl)* Woo, woo! Woo, woo!

BEAUTY: *(laughing)* Oh Beast, you can be so funny sometimes.
I almost forget you're really a sl–
– That you're not. . . as other Masters.

BEAST: If only. . . I once. . . No, I can't tell her.
I know you still can't bear to look at me, Beauty.

BEAUTY: I can take very quick little glances.

BEAST: I do not care to look at myself. I am loathsome.

BEAUTY: You are a little *(whispers)* slug-like.

BEAST: And I do have a slight slime problem.

(The BEAST clicks his fingers. The WILLING HANDS mime mopping him quickly.)

BEAUTY: But you cope with the problem splendidly.
You're very careful not to give offence.

(The BEAST holds out his hand to the WILLING HANDS for another wipe.)

BEAST: *(to WILLING HANDS)* Thoroughly, please.

(The BEAST gently takes BEAUTY's hand with his own. BEAUTY shudders but manages to remain holding his hand.)

BEAST: Are you getting to like me just a little, Beauty?

BEAUTY: You've been very kind. And very attentive.
And ever so funny. And I like you a lot.
(sadly) But I can never marry you, Beast.

BEAST: But I love you.

BEAUTY: *(gently)* I know.

BEAST: I love you even if you're not quite as beautiful
as you were when you first came to my palace.
You are still my beautiful Beauty, but you're so pale
and thin and you have such shadows under your eyes.

BEAUTY: It's because I can't eat and I can't sleep.
I miss my father and my sisters so much.
I do so want to go home.

BEAST: If I keep you here do you think you can
ever ever love me enough to marry me?

BEAUTY:	You know I can never never love you, Beast.
BEAST:	Then go. Now. Before I change my mind. Mount my magic steed and. . .
BEAUTY:	You mean I can go home?
BEAST:	I love you more than I love myself. So go.
ONE:	Go!
TWO:	Go!
THREE, FOUR, FIVE:	Go, go, go!
SIX:	Go!
BUSHES:	*(in whispers)* Go, go, go!

(BEAUTY manages to peck the BEAST on the cheek, then runs off stage. The BEAST groans and sinks to his knees. He clutches his heart.)

BEAST:	*(gasping)* My heart is broken!

(All exit.)

Act 2, Scene 3 – Home Once More

The Merchant's Bedroom. The MERCHANT is lying in bed.
GRACE and MELODY are sitting by him.

BEAUTY: *(running on stage)* Father! Grace! Melody! I'm home!

MERCHANT: My Beauty! I thought I'd never see you again!

GRACE: Beauty! You've come back!

MELODY: We didn't think we'd ever see you again!

MERCHANT: I feel better already.

GRACE: I think it's our nursing, Father.

MELODY: And our chicken soup.

BEAUTY: Oh, I'm so happy to be home.
What a dear kind Beast to set me free.

MERCHANT: That Beast. . . dear? And kind?

GRACE: What has she been up to?

MELODY: She sounds as if she likes the Beast.

BEAUTY: I do. I do like him. Very very much. I just can never love him. So I can't marry him. Poor Beast.

(BEAUTY clutches her heart.)

MERCHANT: What is it, Beauty?

BEAUTY: Nothing, Father. It's just. . .

MERCHANT: You're weary and hungry after your journey.
Grace, Melody, prepare a homecoming feast for your sister.

GRACE: Just like that?

MELODY: Well, you can jolly well help, Beauty.

BEAUTY: Of course I'll help. I'll do everything. I'm just so happy to be home. We can all live happily ever after now. Except the Beast.

(BEAUTY suddenly doubles up with pain, hands crossed over her heart.)

BEAUTY: *(gasping)* Oh Beast!

GRACE: *(to MELODY)* What's she playing at now? She's not really ill, is she?

MELODY: We're not nursing Beauty as well as Father!

BEAUTY: My poor dear Beast.

MERCHANT: Forget that loathsome Beast, Beauty.

BEAUTY: But I can't forget him, Father.
(She doubles up again.)
Oh the pain!

MERCHANT: Where's the pain, Beauty?

BEAUTY: It's in my heart. But it's his heart. The Beast's heart is breaking. Oh Beast! I can't bear it.

(BEAUTY picks herself up, as if to depart.)

MERCHANT: *(alarmed)* Where are you going, Beauty?

BEAUTY: The Beast! My Beast! I'm so scared he'll die of his broken heart. I must go!

(All exit.)

Act 2, Scene 4 – Love Conquers All

The Rose Garden. The BEAST is lying motionless on the ground, clutching his chest. The BUSHES stand in a row, but they are drooping. All the WILLING HANDS are gathered around the BEAST. BEAUTY runs on stage.

BEAUTY: *(She throws herself on her knees.)* Oh Beast!
You let me go because you loved me.
Oh dear sweet wonderful Beast! It wasn't until
you let me go that I realised. I like being with you.
I want to stay here. Oh please don't let it be too late.
Don't die! Please, please don't die!
(She kisses him.) I love you so. . .

BEAST: *(weakly)* You love me, Beauty?

BEAUTY: Yes! I do love you. I don't care what you look like.
I don't care if you're covered in slime. You're my
sweet slimy sluggy Beast and I'll love you forever.
Let us get married!

BEAST: And I'll love you forever too, my Beauty!

(The WILLING HANDS gather round him. He removes his BEAST costume and emerges, as a handsome prince.)

BEAUTY: *(astonished)* My Beast?

BEAST: My Beauty! I was once haughty to an ugly old witch
– and she put a spell on me in return. She condemned me
to creep like a slug and live in my own slime
until the most beautiful girl in the land would marry me.

(BEAUTY and the BEAST kiss. All the WILLING HANDS clap, and the BUSHES wave joyfully.)

SIX: *(terribly excited)* And so Beauty and the Beast
are going to get married!

(WILLING HANDS FIVE and SIX bustle about fetching a crown for the BEAST and a wedding veil for BEAUTY.)

(The BUSHES start singing a wedding song to the tune of Lavender's Blue. The actors playing the GATE come on stage.)

BUSHES: *Roses are red, dilly dilly*
Our Master was green
Now he's a Prince, dilly dilly
And Beauty's his Queen.

BEAUTY: I want everyone to come to my wedding. Father!

(The MERCHANT comes on stage through the GATE and takes a bow.)

BEAUTY: Grace and Melody!

(GRACE and MELODY come on stage through the GATE and bow.)

BEAUTY: *(giggling)* Cupid?

(The MARBLE STATUE comes on and takes a bow.)

BEAUTY: Stand here in the wonderful rose garden.

(She gestures while all the BUSHES take their bow.)

BEAUTY: All the Willing Hands are here. One!

(ONE takes a bow.)

BEAUTY: Two!

(TWO takes a bow.)

BEAUTY: Three, Four, Five!

(THREE, FOUR and FIVE take a bow.)

BEAUTY: And Six!

(SIX takes a bow and claps.)

BEAUTY: And my dear Prince Beast.

(The BEAST takes a bow.)

BEAST: My sweet Beauty.

(BEAUTY bows to him in return.)

BEAUTY: Let's celebrate our wedding – and then we'll all live. . .

ENTIRE CAST and AUDIENCE: Happily Ever After!

(The entire cast sings together, a reprise of the song.)

ALL: *Roses are red, dilly dilly*
Violets are blue
Love conquers all, dilly dilly
Now our play is through!

THE END

Staging

Area for Performance

The word staging implies that you've got a stage! Not all schools have got halls with stages. Not all schools have got *halls*. If you've only got your classroom then you're going to be a little more cramped but you could still put all the chairs and tables at the back of the room (plus any audience). Then the children can act the play in the space that's left. In these circumstances, elaborate props and scenery will only get in the way. Maybe you'll need to halve the number of Willing Hands. The Bushes will have to be lined up next to each other, to form a solid hedge, or they'll be forever bumping into each other. But it *can* be done!

If you've got a hall and you can use it then obviously it's the most suitable setting for the play. If you haven't got a built-in stage, then you'll have to define your acting area. You can make a raised stage with special stage blocks. If these aren't available, mark out the acting area with masking tape. You should do this at the very first rehearsal in the hall, so that the children will get to know the space.

Your area might look something like this:

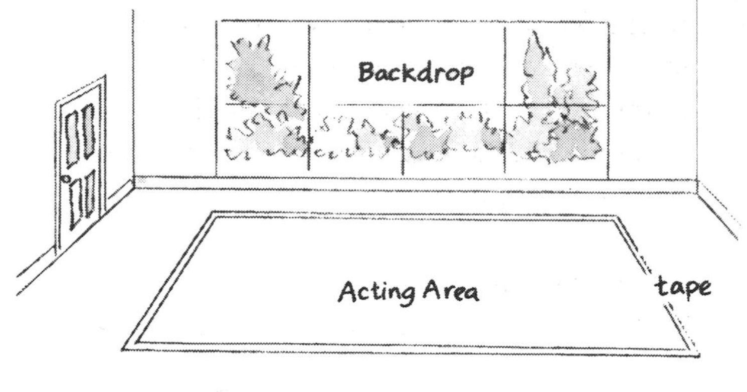

You will need to establish a place where the cast can sit while they are not needed on stage. And, of course, there's got to be room for the props table, the sound effects person, the prompter – and you!

Backdrops

It isn't strictly necessary to have backdrops. The actors themselves – whether they are representing the bushes in Beauty's garden, or rose bushes, or the gate outside the palace – will indicate the location of the scene to the audience. But you might like to make one general purpose backdrop, showing a garden, which could remain in place throughout the play. You should establish the size of the backdrop that you need, and how to hang or display it at the back of the acting area. Stick a number of pieces of paper together with strong tape to make the backdrop and then paint in the colour. Purples, yellows, browns and blues will create a nice 'green' effect from a distance.

Scenery and Props

There are eight scenes in *Beauty and the Beast*. These take place in four locations: in Beauty's garden, outside the palace of the Beast, in the Beast's rose garden, and in the Merchant's bedroom. There are a few extra props to make for the Willing Hands and one special prop for the two actors who represent the gate in the two scenes set outside the palace.

Beauty's Garden
The Bushes in the first scene need to be identified as lilac, lime, lavender, thyme and so on, by different flower badges (see Costume; page 47). The Bushes should stand in a semi-circle throughout this scene, to create Beauty's formal garden.

The Marble Statue appears in the scenes in Beauty's garden. He can be seated during Act 1, scene 1, but needs to stand during Act 1, scene 4. He needs something sturdy to sit on (an old tea chest would be suitable). It should be painted white.

Outside the Palace
The two actors who represent the gate need an actual gate which they can open. It is quite simple to make the gate. You will need a piece of material (such as an old sheet) and two pieces of dowling which should be about two-thirds of the actor's height, in length. The pieces of dowling make the two gate posts. To make the gate, cut the material into a rectangle, making its longest side about two-thirds of the height of the posts. Paint the bars of the gate on to the rectangle of material, and cut out a small key hole. To attach the gate to the two posts, fold each side of the material around each of the posts and staple the material tightly around each post. Staple the material at the top of each post to keep it in position, as shown below.

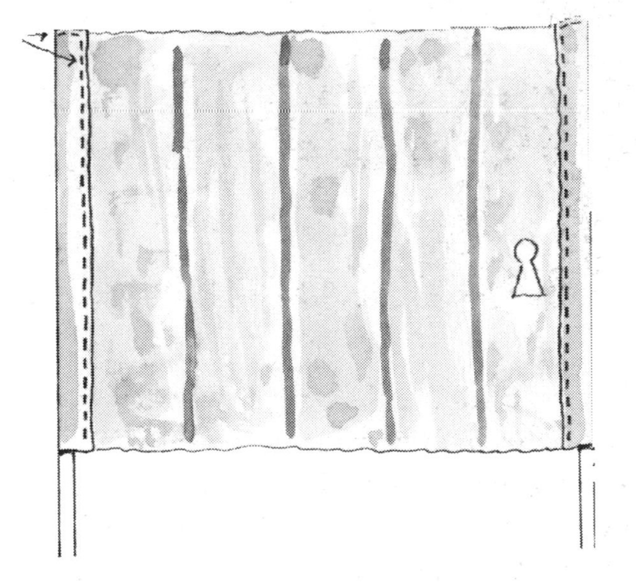

The two actors should hold on to the posts of the gate. When the Merchant is about to enter through the gate, one of the actors should pass the pole of his side of the gate to the other. Then the Merchant can step through!

Scenery and Props

The Rose Garden
In the scenes located in the rose garden, once again the Bushes themselves provide the scenery and show the audience where the action is taking place. Having done a quick change during Act 1, scene 2, they are now Rose Bushes. They have removed their flower badges and transformed themselves by using face paints.

During Act 1, scene 3, the Rose Bushes stand in a semi-circle with their arms linked, to form a hedge. One Rose Bush at the end of the semi-circle should hold a paper rose in their free hand. The Merchant should pick this rose to take home to Beauty.

The Rose Bushes can sit during Act 2, scene 2. In the final scene, they should stand to form a hedge. This means that they will be on their feet to take their bow at the end of the play.

The Merchant's Bedroom
In this scene (Act 2, scene 3), you will need a bench and a couple of pillows to show the audience that this is the Merchant's bedroom.

Props

Some of the actors will need their own individual props which are listed below. You might like to set up a props table off stage, where all the props will be located. The actors should collect their props from the table, before the beginning of each act.

Act 1, Scene 1
A small dead rose bush in a pot
A trowel and a water spray for Beauty
Act 1, Scene 2
A large golden key for Hand One
and again in Act 2, scene 1
Act 1, Scene 3
A paper rose for one of the Rose Bushes
Act 1, Scene 4
A paper rose in a vase
Act 2, Scene 2
A hankie for Hand One
A large envelope for Hand Two
A book for Hand Three
A fan for Hand Four
A piece of jewellery for Hand Five
A cloak to cover the Beast for Hand Six
Act 2, Scene 3
A bowl and spoon for Melody
Act 2, Scene 4
A crown for the Beast for Hand Five
A wedding veil for Beauty for Hand Six

Some of these props are easy to find, but others need to be made. The actors might like to make or find their own props. Here are some suggestions:

A large golden key
Cut a key shape out from strong card, and paint it gold.

Scenery and Props

A paper rose
You will need stem wire, and card or tissue paper. Cut out six or seven flower shapes from the card or paper. Then make two holes in the middle of each flower shape. Lay all the flower shapes on top of each other. Use the wire to make the stem and thread it up through the first hole and down through the second hole, as shown below. Bind the wire around underneath the flower shapes to hold them in place.

A large envelope with a letter inside
You could write the letter from the Beast on to a piece of card (see page 24 of the playscript). You can use this template below to make the envelope. Fold flaps B and D towards each other, and glue flap C on top of both. Tuck in flap A to close the envelope.

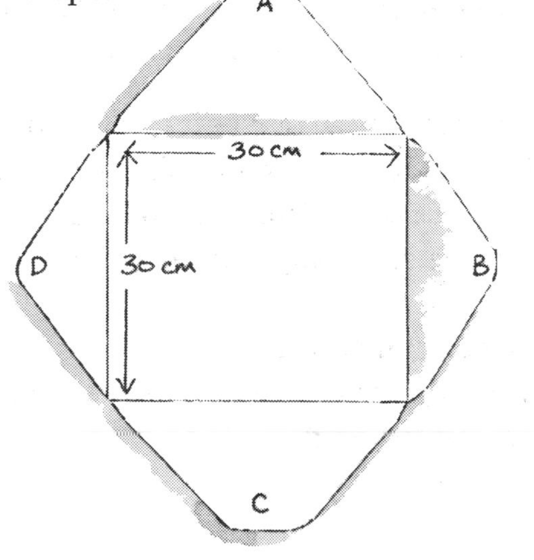

A piece of jewellery
You could make a necklace by threading buttons, old plastic beads, or pieces of macaroni, on to strong thread. Or you might like to make a brooch. Cut a circle or diamond shape from card to make a base. Scrunch up some scrap paper. Make a little mound of scrap paper and fix it to the base with masking tape. Paint the brooch gold and decorate it with sequins. Fasten a safety pin to the back of the brooch with tape.

A cloak to cover the Beast
A cloak can be made from a piece of old material. Make small cuts in the top of the piece of material, and thread it through with ribbon to make a drawstring.

A crown for the Beast
Cut a 15cm wide strip of card and fit it to the actor's head. Staple the ends to join them together. Cut zig-zag shapes into the top of the crown. Paint it gold and glue scrunched-up sweet papers on to the crown for the 'jewels'.

A wedding veil for Beauty
A square of old net curtain, or a light Indian cotton scarf, would make a very suitable veil for Beauty.

Lighting

If your school has a proper stage you may have theatrical lighting as well, with floodlights and spots – *and* an adult who knows how to work them, who can supervise this. If so, you can follow the lighting directions within the playscript. If not, you could switch the hall lights off and then on again to good effect during Act 2, scene 2, where night is followed by dawn.

Casting and Auditions

Allocating the Roles

You're going to get a lot of children wanting to be Beauty or the Beast. They may be very determined! They will wave their hands at you and beg to be picked. Some of them will smile dazzlingly at you and others will make exaggerated Beast faces. The shy and the surly will slide down in their seats, not wanting to be Beauty or the Beast or anyone else for that matter. The super-cool kids will raise their eyebrows and sigh and go 'Boring!' The always-in-trouble brigade at the back of the class won't even have been listening but when they eventually find out what's going on they'll say 'Well, bet we don't get picked, it's not *fair*!'

Somehow you've got to get it across to the children that the production is for everyone. There are all sorts of parts. If someone has a big part then they're going to have to learn lots of lines and that's hard work. So it might be more fun to have a small part. Any musicians or talented artists are going to be vital to the play. There has to be a reliable quick-witted stage management team. Everyone will take part in one way or another – and at least you can plant a large number of Bushes on stage so that every single child who wants to act can do so.

The class cynic might mutter that you'll still pick your favourites for the *best* parts. The good readers. The clever clogs. You'll have to explain that no actors get picked just like that. They have to *audition*. . .

Casting and Auditions

The Auditions

You may have produced plays before and have your own ideas about how to structure the auditions. But if you haven't, you may find these suggestions helpful.

There are twelve speaking parts in *Beauty and the Beast*, an entire garden of Bushes who chant and sing occasionally, and two more actors who play the Gate. Before you do anything else, I suggest that you talk to the children about the story of this play. It might be a very different rendering from the one they know from an old fairytale book at home. If they've seen the Walt Disney film they'll be expecting talking teapots. It would be helpful to talk about the characters themselves as well (see pages 42 – 43 for descriptions). Then they will have some idea of the play before you begin the group audition.

• First of all, you will want the children to quieten down and concentrate. Ask them to stand absolutely still as the Marble Statue.

• Ask them to improvise and to mime some simple actions: swaying in the breeze as a Rose Bush; opening an imaginary door and looking out of it; and wiping the slime off the Beast with imaginary mops.

• Then you could ask for something a little more difficult: get them to show you their reaction when they come face to face with a slug far bigger than themselves!

• Next, make them work in pairs. One should play the Merchant, the other the Beast. Ask them to improvise the first meeting of the Merchant with the Beast (during Act 1, sc. 3). After that, each pair of actors should swop roles.

• Divide the children up into sets of four. Ask them to do some role playing, with one child acting the part of the parent, and the three others as the quarrelling siblings. This will show you how children act with each other in a group, and might well help you to cast the Willing Hands!

• Once this session has been completed, you will have some idea of the different children's abilities. You will be able to see who is really interested and willing to concentrate on the job in hand. Then you could give out scripts of particular scenes for a 'read through'.

• At the read through, organise the children into groups, and ask them to read through some scenes. If a child becomes very nervous and stuttery, allow them to try again, before making any final decisions. Hopefully you'll be able to offer all the children eager to be involved some kind of role, even if it's not a major speaking part.

The Main Characters

Beauty
A loyal and loving girl.
She can be timid, but has great courage.

The Beast
Arrogant, proud, and sometimes vain. He is also very kind and comes to love Beauty deeply.

The Prince
Once the spell has been broken, the Beast becomes a charming prince.

The Merchant
A middle-aged widower, down on his luck.
Well-meaning, but weak.

Melody
The middle sister.
Sharp-tongued and indignant.
She is musical.

Grace
The older sister.
Very bossy and self-important.
She's graceful and light on her feet.

The Marble Statue
Has a very high opinion of himself – a cut above all other garden statues!

The Willing Hands
The servants of the Beast.

One
Has the air of a head butler.

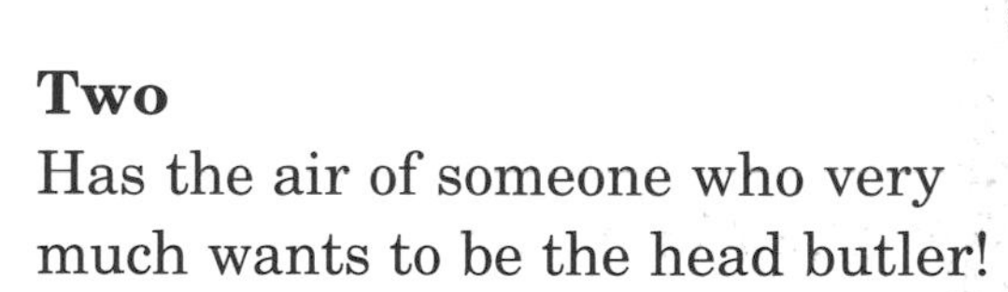

Two
Has the air of someone who very much wants to be the head butler!

Three, Four and Five
They do everything together and usually talk in unison.

Six
Always dashing about – never there at the right moment!

The Stage Management Team

You might like to start by emphasizing how important a good stage management team is to a successful production of the play, and stress that this is a vital role. Then you could ask who might be interested in being involved, or who is keen to have the status of Director's Assistant. You should have plenty of takers after that! The stage management team should attend rehearsals from the beginning.

Director's Assistant
Your Willing Hand. Involve your assistant as much as possible in the decisions you make about the production. Choose someone you can rely on to take messages, find things out, and to remind you of what still needs to be done.

Lighting
An adult is required to supervise the use of theatrical lighting. In this case, he or she might find an assistant very useful. If you are not using theatrical lighting, one person should have responsibility for turning the ceiling lights on and off during scene changes, and at appropriate moments during the play.

Props Table
One person should be in charge of the props table. He or she should make a list of the props required for Act 1 and Act 2 (see page 38) and make sure that these props are on the table before the beginning of each act.

Prompter
A very important role. The prompter should be seated off stage with their own copy of the playscript, ready to tell the actors their lines, if necessary.

Sound Effects
Two members of the team could divide up the sound effects between them. They should each have a copy of the playscript, with their individual cues highlighted.

Scene Shifters
Two people are needed to be in charge of putting up the backdrop, and carrying large props on and off stage. They should wear dark-coloured clothes.

Front of House
Two members of the team could organise the seating, show the audience to their seats, and give out programmes.

Rehearsal Schedule

It's a good idea to fix a firm date for the Grand Performance as soon as possible, so that you can all work towards it. You should then decide how many rehearsals you'll need, including a technical rehearsal (where all the members of the stage management team practise their individual roles).

You should also have a dress rehearsal (a full run through of the play with everything in place except the audience). If the children will be required to attend lunchtime or after-school rehearsals, you should make it plain that they are expected to be very prompt, in a professional way.

Costume

This is the interesting bit! The first dress rehearsal always rekindles acting enthusiasm. It's most important that the actors feel comfortable in their costumes, and can speak their lines and move about easily. Costumes don't have to be elaborate to look very effective on stage. You will need to ask parents if their children can bring in T-shirts, or bodies and leggings, to be used as part of their costume. (These clothes can be returned after the performance.) Other parts of the costume can be made quite easily. Here are some ideas:

Female Roles

Beauty and her sisters can get away with wearing anything simple and decorative. If you can borrow a long full skirt and a simple white blouse, she will look very traditional. A wide belt would complete her costume. To make one, cut a strip of thin cardboard (10 cm wide) and fit it around the actress's waist. You could paint the belt gold or silver, or cover it with silver foil. Staple or tape it at the back to fasten it together.

Beauty
Alternatively, you could give Beauty a more modern look, by teaming up a leotard or body, with a bubblewrap skirt. Bubblewrap is light but bulky, so it makes a nicely full skirt. First, cut a piece of elastic (about an inch wide) to fit Beauty's waist, then gather the pieces of bubblewrap together at the top. Tack them loosely to the elastic waistband.

Staple the pieces of bubblewrap together at the sides. You could glue glitter or sequins on to the skirt to decorate it.

Grace and Melody
Grace and Melody wear similar costumes to Beauty. They should all wear differently coloured belts, or they could decorate their bubblewrap skirts individually. Ordinary shoes, or gym shoes, can be made to look glamorous, by dressing them up with ribbon or tinsel.

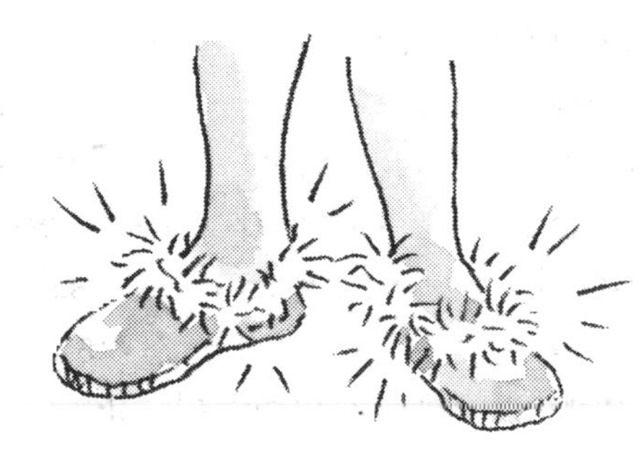

Costume

Male Roles

Merchant
The Merchant needs to look older than the other characters. Dark leggings, and a white shirt turned back to front form the basis of his costume. He could wear a loosely knotted scarf around his neck and a long jacket or coat. You might like to give him a beard with face paints.

The Beast
You can have fun with him! To begin with, he needs a black or dark green sweatshirt top and leggings, socks and gym shoes. Use a hairband and pipe cleaners to make the Beast's feelers, as shown opposite.

To make his slug frill, first find a large black plastic sack. Cut off the bottom end. Then cut it open up one side and lay the whole piece of black plastic out flat. Smooth out the folds. Then fold it in half and pin it up the right-hand side.

Next, cut the double thickness of plastic into a square. The length of each side of the square should be the same as the length of the actor's arm from neck to wrist.

Fold the top left-hand corner to the bottom right-hand corner to make a triangle shape and pin it along the bottom edge.

Look at the diagram, then take side A over to side B and pin the two together.

You will get a shape that looks like this. Cut off the small triangle.

Cut a wavy pattern into side C.

Open out the slug frill. Use tape or safety pins to attach the long straight edge to the backs of the actor's arms.

When the Beast becomes a prince (see page 33 of the playscript) the Willing Hands should gather round him to take off his slug frill and feelers, and put on his crown!

Marble Statue
The Marble Statue represents Cupid. He could wear a white or pale grey top and leggings. Cupid could be identified by sticking a red heart shape on his top. You could easily cut this out of adhesive-backed plastic.

Costume

Unisex Roles

Willing Hands

The Willing Hands should be dressed all in black. Leggings and tops or leotards and tights would be suitable. They should not wear shoes. Alternatively, their costumes can be made from an old sheet, dyed black. Measure the actor's height from knee to shoulder. Cut out a rectangle twice that length from the sheet. Fold it in half, then measure the size of the actor's head, and cut out an opening for their neck. Sew up the sides and the costume is complete.

Tie it at the waist with cord.

The Willing Hands' hands need to look magical. You could buy some silver sticky tape (the sort for wrapping Christmas presents) and stick it along the backs of their fingers and thumb.

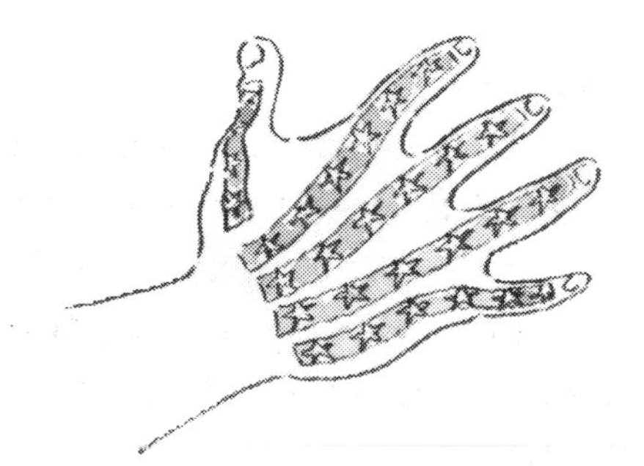

The Bushes

The actors should all wear dark-coloured clothes; green, black, brown or dark blue would all be suitable. Or you could make them a costume from a dyed sheet, in the same way as for the Willing Hands. When the actors are required to be the Bushes in Beauty's garden, they should wear flower badges to show which kind of bush or tree they represent. Cut a flower shape out of card. Paint it the appropriate colour for the flower of that particular bush. Fasten a bar pin brooch to the back.

During Act 1, scene 2, the Bushes should transform themselves into Rose Bushes by removing their flower badges and painting roses on to their faces with make up.

The Gate

It might be fun for these two actors to look quite menacing. Black jeans or trousers and T-shirts would be ideal for their costume. They could also wear black balaclavas, or black hairbands with silver foil spikes glued on top.

Music

The Bushes sing several songs, but they're all written to accompany the same tune, 'Lavender's Blue'. If you've got a school orchestra or a group of competent musicians they can accompany the Bushes, and play suitably dark and menacing music during Act 1, scene 3 – Strange Meetings. If this is over-estimating everyone's musical ability then a snatch of taped music here and there is very effective. You could bring one of those classic compilation tapes in to the classroom and get the children to listen with you to see what might be useful for the play.

Dances

There's one dance at the end of the play which can be as simple or elaborate as you wish. You could organise a simple country dance. All the actors will need to join up in pairs. Then the couples should face each other, right hands joined and held aloft, stepping in a stately fashion to the right, and then to the left. Alternatively, you could teach a waltz to the music of 'Lavender's Blue'. The Gay Gordons also fits the music and is enjoyably boisterous and easy to learn.

Sound Effects

This play calls for various sound effects. Here are some suggestions about how you might achieve them.

Footsteps = knock a block of wood on the floor
Thunder = shake sheets of flexible cardboard
Horses' hooves = knock half-coconut shells or flowerpots together
Strange tinkling music = strike a triangle or chime bar in quick rhythm
A knock at the door = rap a block of wood on a table top
Horses' neigh = the sound effects people should practise this!

You might prefer to invent your own sound effects, and record them. Then you can use a tape recorder to reproduce them on the night.

Anything Else?

Everyone will get het up and nervous before the big performance. You may occasionally wish that you'd never got involved in putting on the whole thing. But nothing beats the fun and excitement of putting on a show, and you will doubtless have a big hit on the night. You could tell your cast and stage management team that it's weirdly considered bad luck to wish each other good luck. In the theatre they say 'Break a leg!' instead.